Dear Parent:
Your child's love of reading starts here!

Every child learns to read in a different way and at his or her own speed. Some go back and forth between reading levels and read favorite books again and again. Others read through each level in order. You can help your young reader improve and become more confident by encouraging his or her own interests and abilities. From books your child reads with you to the first books he or she reads alone, there are I Can Read Books for every stage of reading:

SHARED READING
Basic language, word repetition, and whimsical illustrations, ideal for sharing with your emergent reader

BEGINNING READING
Short sentences, familiar words, and simple concepts for children eager to read on their own

READING WITH HELP
Engaging stories, longer sentences, and language play for developing readers

READING ALONE
Complex plots, challenging vocabulary, and high-interest topics for the independent reader

ADVANCED READING
Short paragraphs, chapters, and exciting themes for the perfect bridge to chapter books

I Can Read Books have introduced children to the joy of reading since 1957. Featuring award-winning authors and illustrators and a fabulous cast of beloved characters, I Can Read Books set the standard for beginning readers.

A lifetime of discovery begins with the magical words "I Can Read!"

Visit www.icanread.com for information
on enriching your child's reading experience.

Biscuit

story by ALYSSA SATIN CAPUCILLI
pictures by PAT SCHORIES

HarperCollins*Publishers*

HarperCollins®, 🐾®, and I Can Read Book® are trademarks of HarperCollins Publishers Inc.

Library of Congress Cataloging-in-Publication Data
Capucilli, Alyssa Satin.
  Biscuit / story by Alyssa Satin Capucilli ; pictures by Pat Schories.
    p.   cm. — (An I can read book)
  Summary: A little yellow dog wants ever one more thing before he'll go to sleep.
  ISBN-10: 0-06-026197-8 (trade bdg.) — ISBN-13: 978-0-06-026197-9 (trade bdg.)
  ISBN-10: 0-06-026198-6 (lib. bdg.) — ISBN-13: 978-0-06-026198-6 (lib. bdg.)
  ISBN-10: 0-06-444212-8 (pbk.) — ISBN-13: 978-0-06-444212-1 (pbk.)
  [1. Dogs—Fiction. 2. Bedtime—Fiction.] I. Schories, Pat, ill. II. Title. III. Series.
PZ7.C179Bi 1997   95-9716
[E]—dc20   CIP
                                                                                                       AC

❖

For Laura and Peter who wait patiently
for a Biscuit of their very own
—A. S. C.

For Tess
—P. S.

This is Biscuit.

Biscuit is small.

Biscuit is yellow.

Time for bed, Biscuit!

6

Woof, woof!

Biscuit wants to play.

Time for bed, Biscuit!

Woof, woof!

Biscuit wants a snack.

8

Time for bed, Biscuit!

Woof, woof!

Biscuit wants a drink.

Time for bed, Biscuit!

Woof, woof!

Biscuit wants to hear a story.

Time for bed, Biscuit!

Woof, woof!

Biscuit wants his blanket.

Time for bed, Biscuit!

Woof, woof!

Biscuit wants his doll.

Time for bed, Biscuit!

Woof, woof!

Biscuit wants a hug.

Time for bed, Biscuit!

Woof, woof!

Biscuit wants a kiss.

Time for bed, Biscuit!

Woof, woof!

Biscuit wants a light on.

Woof!

Biscuit wants to be tucked in.

Woof!

Biscuit wants one more kiss.

Woof!

Biscuit wants one more hug.

Woof!

Biscuit wants to curl up.

23

Sleepy puppy.

Good night, Biscuit.